NICKELODEON

D0449539

SpongeBob SquarePants™

TALES FROM BIKINI BOTTOM

Contributing Editor - Paul Morrissey
Design, Layout and Lettering - Dave Snow
Cover Layout - Raymond Makowski
Production Specialist - Tomás Montalvo-Lagos

Editor - Elizabeth Hurchalla
Managing Editor - Jill Freshney
Production Coordinator - Antonio DePietro
Production Manager - Jennifer Miller
Art Director - Matt Alford
Editorial Director - Jeremy Ross
VP of Production & Manufacturing - Ron Klamert
President & C.O.O. - John Parker
Publisher & C.E.O. - Stuart Levy

Come visit us online at www.TOKYOPOP.com

A TOKYOPOP® Cine-Manga™
TOKYOPOP Inc.
5900 Wilshire Blvd., Suite 2000, Los Angeles, CA 90036

SpongeBob SquarePants Tales from Bikini Bottom

ISBN: 1-59182-575-X
First TOKYOPOP® printing: February 2004

10 9 8 7 6 5 4 3 2

Printed in Canada

NICKELODEON

SpongeBob SquarePants™

Created by Stephen Hillenburg

TALES FROM BIKINI BOTTOM

TOKYOPOP®

LOS ANGELES • TOKYO • LONDON

SPONGEBOB SQUAREPANTS: An optimistic and friendly sea sponge who lives in a pineapple with his snail, Gary, and works as a fry cook at The Krusty Krab. He loves his job and is always looking on the bright side of everything.

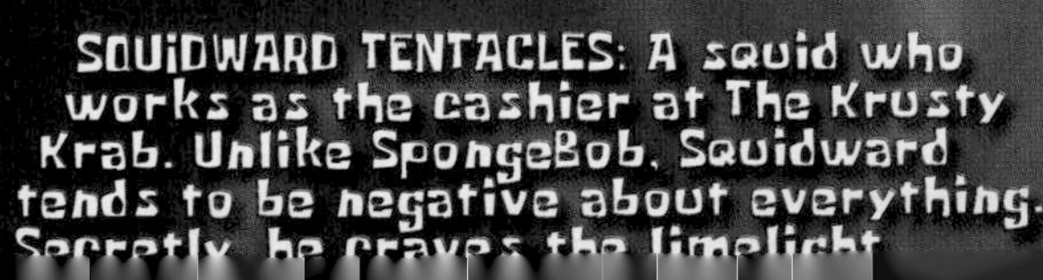

SQUIDWARD TENTACLES: A squid who works as the cashier at The Krusty Krab. Unlike SpongeBob, Squidward tends to be negative about everything. Secretly, he craves the limelight.

MR. KRABS: A crab who owns and runs The Krusty Krab. Mr. Krabs loves money and will do anything to avoid losing it. Mr. Krabs also adores his daughter, Pearl.

GARY: SpongeBob's pet snail. Meows like a cat.

PLANKTON: A plankton who constantly sneaks into The Krusty Krab attempting to get his hands on a famous Krabby Patty. Despite his size, Plankton can be a big threat to Mr. Krabs.

SANDY: A thrill-seeking squirrel who loves SpongeBob as much as she loves eXtreme sports.

PATRICK STAR: A starfish who is SpongeBob's best friend and neighbor.

TALES FROM BIKINI BOTTOM

SpongeBob
SquarePants
™
Home Sweet
Pineapple
by Ennio Torresan, Jr., Erik Wiese
and Mr. Lawrence

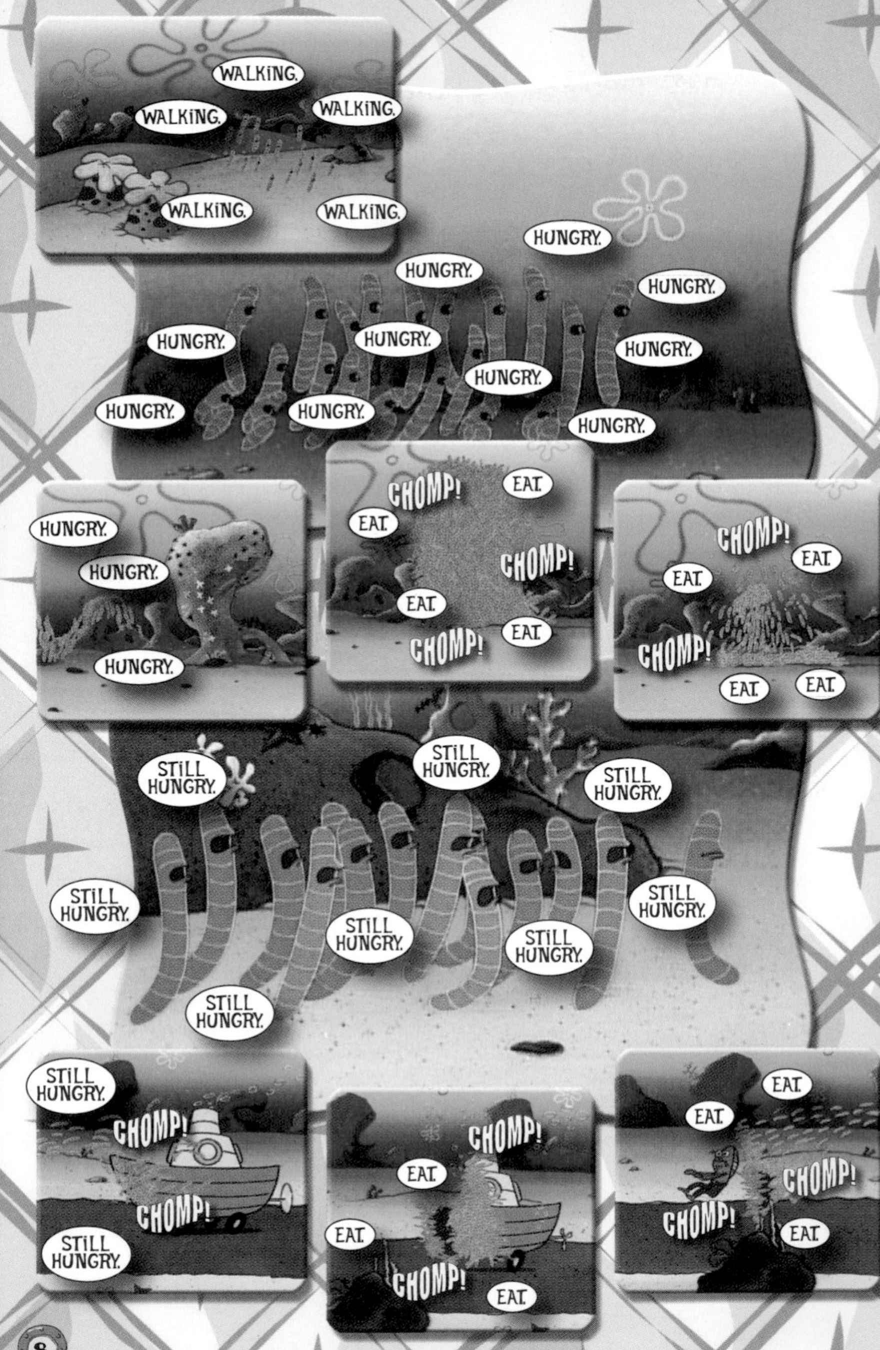
WALKING.
WALKING.
WALKING.
WALKING.
WALKING.
HUNGRY.
HUNGRY.
HUNGRY.
HUNGRY.
HUNGRY.
HUNGRY.
HUNGRY.
HUNGRY.
HUNGRY.
HUNGRY.
HUNGRY.
HUNGRY.
HUNGRY.
CHOMP!
EAT.
EAT.
CHOMP!
EAT.
CHOMP!
EAT.
CHOMP!
EAT.
EAT.
CHOMP!
EAT.
EAT.
STILL HUNGRY.
STILL HUNGRY.
STILL HUNGRY.
STILL HUNGRY.
STILL HUNGRY.
STILL HUNGRY.
STILL HUNGRY.
STILL HUNGRY.
STILL HUNGRY.
CHOMP!
CHOMP!
STILL HUNGRY.
CHOMP!
EAT.
EAT.
CHOMP!
EAT.
EAT.
EAT.
CHOMP!
CHOMP!
EAT.

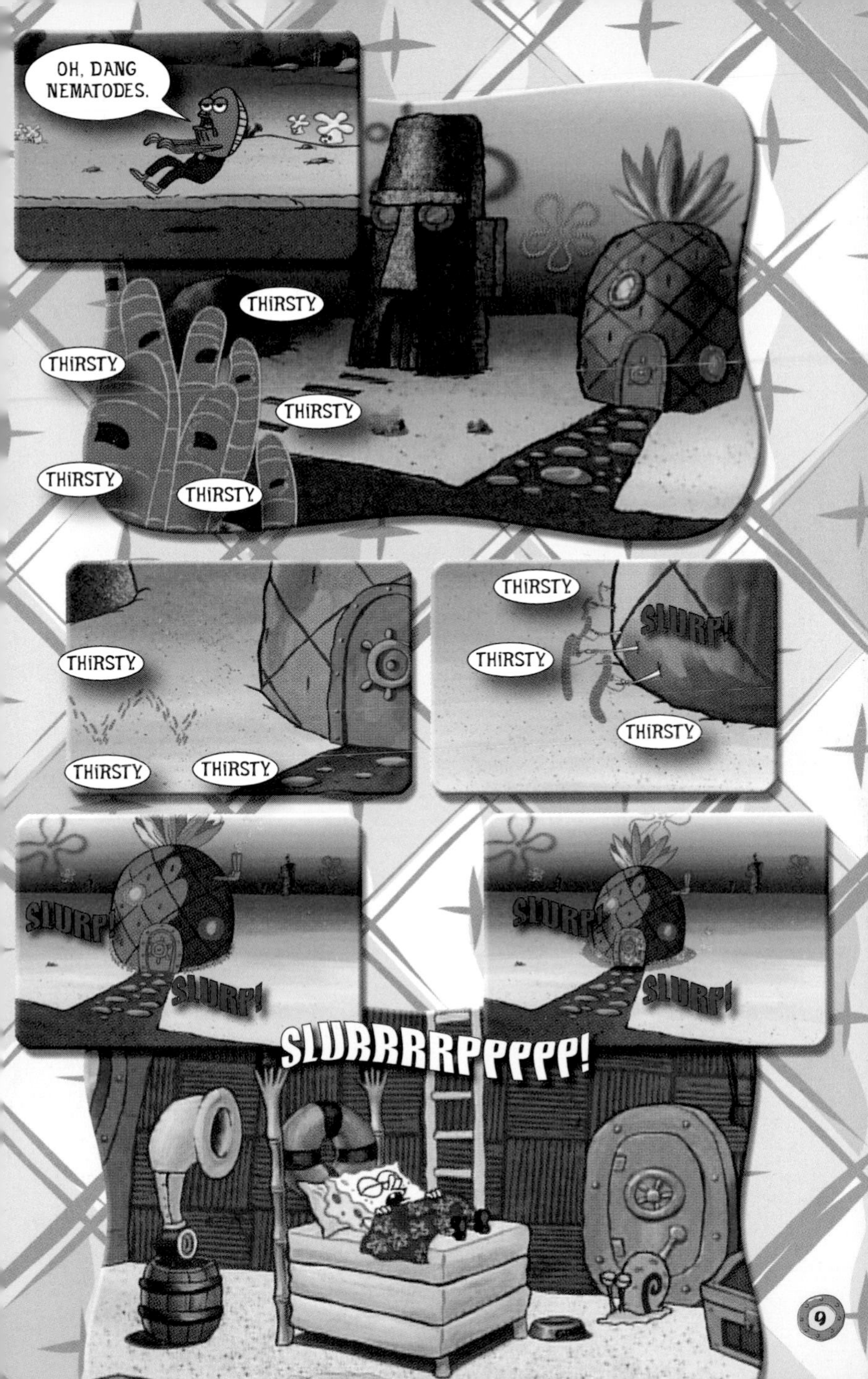
OH, DANG NEMATODES.
THIRSTY.
THIRSTY.
THIRSTY.
THIRSTY.
THIRSTY.
THIRSTY.
THIRSTY.
THIRSTY.
THIRSTY.
THIRSTY.
SLURP!
THIRSTY.
SLURP!
SLURP!
SLURP!
SLURP!
SLURRRRPPPPP!

SLURRRRPPPPP!

SLURRRRPPPPP!

MEOW!

SLURRRRPPPPP!

SLURRRRPPPPP!

HURRAY, GARY!
WE'RE FINALLY
HUGE!

HUH?
WAIT A MINUTE!
OH NO!

SHHH-POP!

SLURRRRPPPPP!

SLURRRRPPPPPP!
MEOW!
OH, SHELL PHONE! I KNOW! I'LL CALL SQUIDWARD. HE'LL KNOW WHAT TO DO!
SLURRRRPPPPPP!
HELLO?
SQUIDWARD!
IS IT TIME ALREADY FOR YOU TO RUIN MY DAY?
SQUIDWARD, HELP ME! MY HOUSE IS SHRINKING. I WOKE UP THIS MORNING AND IT WAS GETTING SMALLER...
SLURRRRPPPPPP!
OH NO!
YEP. IT'S TIME.

AIEE-YAH!
HUH? IS IT TIME ALREADY TO RUIN SQUID'S DAY?
HUH?
CREAK!
AAAAK!
OOOF!!!
RUSTLE! RUSTLE!
HEY, SPONGEBOB! DON'T START WITHOUT ME!
SLURP!
SLURP!
SLURP!
SLURP!
SLURP!
SLURP!
BURP
BURP
BURP
BURP

HUH?
NEMATODES!
THE ONLY THING LEFT OF MY HOUSE IS THIS LITTLE PEBBLE.
WHAT'S GOING ON HERE?!
I'VE GOT BAD NEWS, GUYS! LOOK AT WHAT HAPPENED TO MY HOUSE!!! IT'S GONE. IT'S ALL GONE!!!
WHAT AM I GONNA DO? WHERE AM I GOING TO LIVE?
WELL, WHAT CAN I SAY?! IT HAS BEEN GREAT KNOWING YOU, SPONGEBOB.
GOOD LUCK SOMEWHERE ELSE! I'M GONNA MISS YA. BOO-HOO! BOO-HOO!
HA! HA! HA! HA!
SQUID'S TAKIN' IT REAL HARD.

WHAT ARE YOU GONNA DO NOW?
I GUESS I'LL HAVE TO MOVE BACK WITH MY MOM AND DAD...
MOM AND DAD
NAW, WAIT A MINUTE! NO, YOU DON'T! WE CAN BUILD YOU A NEW HOUSE!
MOM AND DAD
WE CAN'T BUILD A WHOLE HOUSE!
WELL, SURE. IT'S EASY. I BUILT MY HOUSE ALL BY MYSELF.
TA-DA!
ALL RIGHT, PATRICK! LET'S GET TO WORK!

OUCH!!!
WHACK!
WHACK!
WHACK!
KRACK!
WOOSH!
OWW!
THUNK!

WE'RE DONE!
YEAH! SO WHAT DO YOU THINK?
i WISH i LIVED THERE!
REALLY?
NO!
ONE BEDROOM!
DOING!

POP
AWWW!
TARTAR SAUCE!!
LOOKS LIKE WE GOTTA MOVE BACK WITH MOM AND POP...
YOU CAN'T MOVE BACK IN WITH YOUR PARENTS! WHEN MY PARENTS KICKED ME OUT OF THE HOUSE, I NEVER WENT BACK!
WAIT! YOU AND GARY CAN COME STAY WITH ME!
THAT WOULD BE GREAT!
YEAH, WE'LL BE ROCK MATES.

GOOD NIGHT, SPONGEBOB!
GOOD NIGHT, ROCK MATE.
KA-BOOM!
OUCH!
GOOD NIGHT, GARY.
MEOW!
SNHOGGH!
ZZZZ!
SHOOOO!
ZZZZ!
SNHOGGH!
ACK!
SHOOOO!
SPOINT

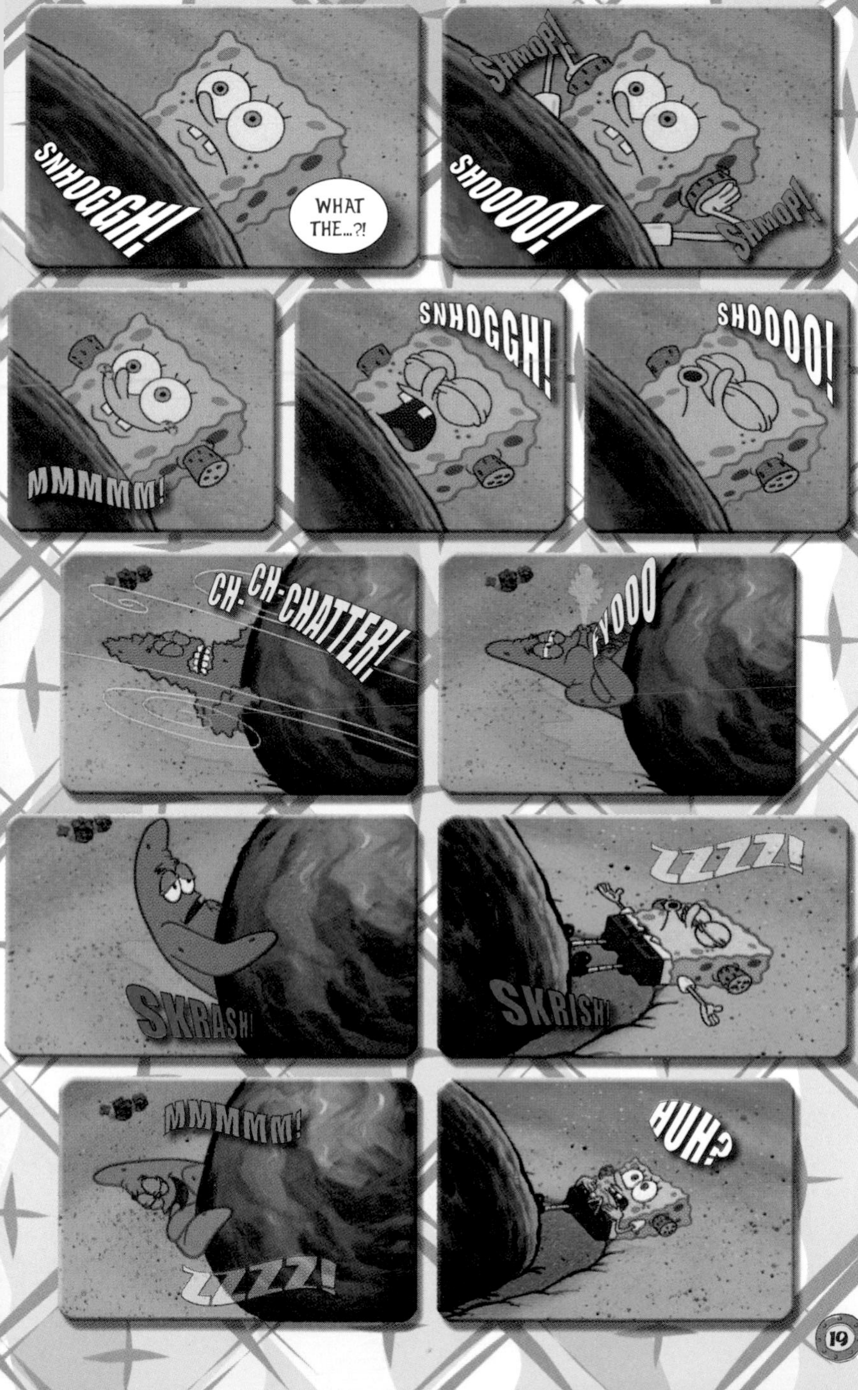

SNHOGGH!
WHAT THE...?!

SHMOP!
SHOOOO!
SHMOP!

MMMMMM!

SNHOGGH!

SHOOOO!

CH-CH-CHATTER!

FYOOO

SKRASH!

ZZZZ!
SKRISH!

MMMMMM!
ZZZZ!

HUH?

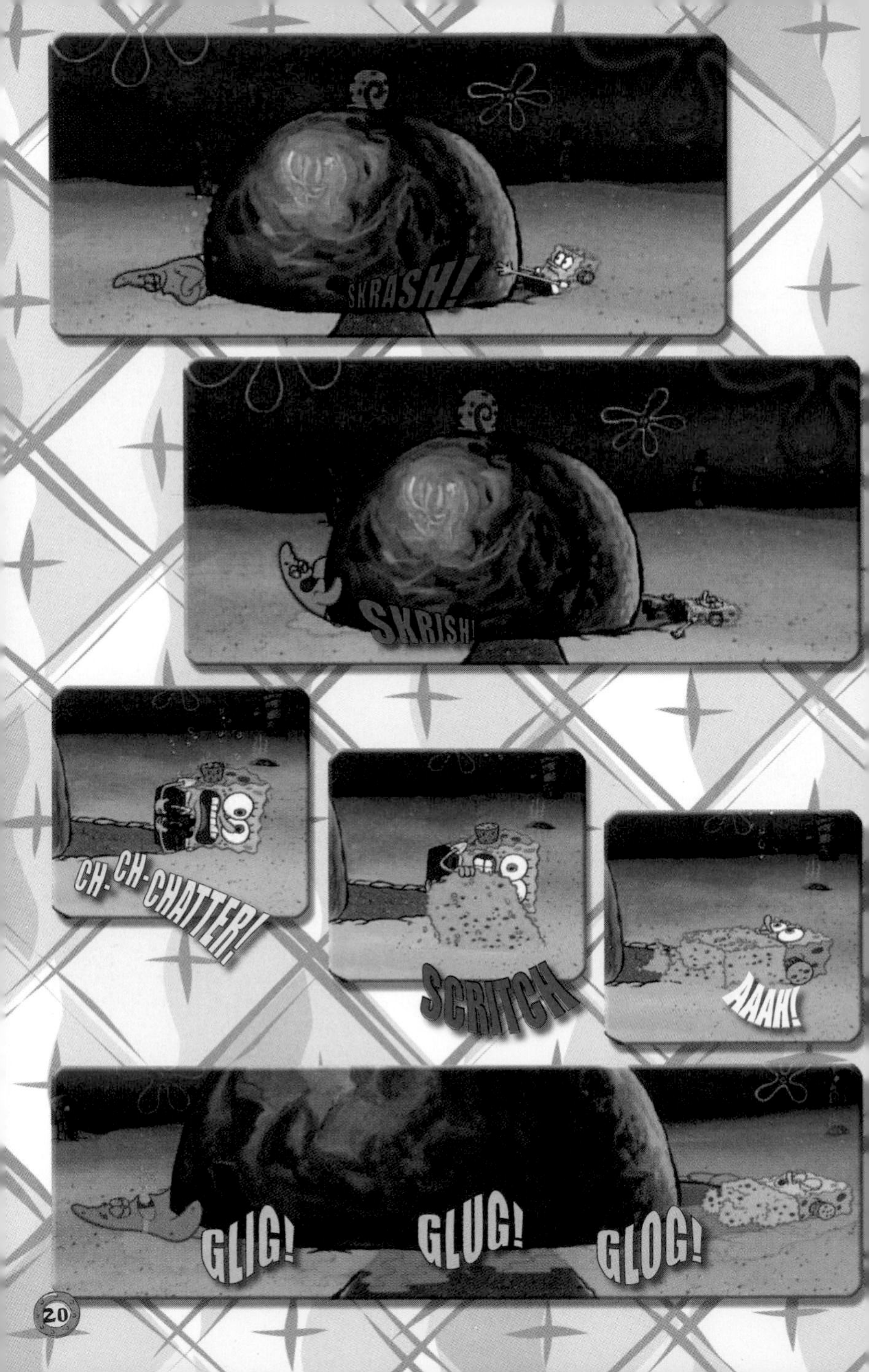
SKRASH!
SKRISH!
CH-CH-CHATTER!
SCRITCH
AAAH!
GLIG!
GLUG!
GLOG!

SHLOOP!
SHHHHHH
SHHHHHH
SCRITCH
MMMMMM!
AAAAAAH!!! SPIDERS!!!! SPIDERS!!! GET 'EM OFF ME! GET 'EM OFF ME!! GET 'EM OFF ME!!!
KA-THUNK!
KA-THUNK!
KA-THUNK!
PATRICK, WAKE UP! IT'S ME, SPONGEBOB.
MOHHOFF OFFOMTHMPRH...

UNGGGGH!
ZZZZ!
SPIDERS!!
SPIDERS!!
SPIDERS!!!
GET 'EM OFF
ME!!!
KA-THUNK!
OW, OW, OW,
OW, OW, OW, OW!
KA-THUNK!
GET 'EM
OFF! GET 'EM OFF!
GET 'EM OFF ME!
KA-THUNK!

TAP!
TAP!
SQUIDWARD?
SQUIDWARD? SQUIDWARD, COULD WE STAY HERE A COUPLE OF DAYS OR A MONTH OR TWO?
YEAH... WHATEVER...
THANKS!!
HMMMMM...
SQUIDWARD, CAN YOU SCOOT OVER A LITTLE?!
I LIKE SLEEPOVERS. THIS IS GREAT. GOOD NIGHT, SQUIDWARD!
GOOD NIGHT, SPONGEBOB.
GOOD NIGHT, SPONGEBOB.

TODAY'S THE BIG DAY, SQUIDWARD. THE DAY SPONGEBOB MOVES!
I CAN'T BELIEVE IT'S REALLY HAPPENING!
DON'T WORRY, SQUIDWARD, I'LL COME VISIT YOU!
DON'T TRY TO CHEER ME UP, SPONGEBOB, PLEASE...
HERE COME MY PARENTS!!
SPONGEBOB! HI, HONEY. WE'RE HERE.
C'MON, SPONGEBOB!
HURRY, SON! YOUR MOTHER HAS DINNER WAITING!

Hi, MOM!
HELLLLLOOO, MRS. SQUAREPANTS! LET ME HELP YOU WiTH THESE BAGS!
i CANNOT HOLD ON TO YOU ANY LONGER, LiTTLE PEBBLE.
YOU HOLD TOO MANY MEMORiES!
SCRATCH!
SCRATCH!
PLOP!
SNIFF

DRIP
PLOP!
SPLASH
KA-ZAM!
WELL, SQUIDWARD, THIS IS GOODBYE.
GOODBYE, SPONGEBOB... GOODBYE.
GOODBYE, SPONGEBOB. BYE, BYE, BYE. GOODBYE. GOODBYE, SPONGEBOB... GOODBYE, SPONGEBOB.

C'MON, SPONGEBOB!!
GOODBYE, PATRICK. GOODBYE, BIKINI BOTTOM!
SOB!
SOB!
SOB!
SOB!
SOB!
SPONGEBOB IS LEAVING! LA LA LA LA LEAVING! HA HA! SPONGEBOB IS LEAVING, HE'S LEAVING.
ZAMMO!
SPLITCH! SPLATCH!
KOOOOOSH!
SPLOOSH!!

SPROING!
THUNK!
MY HOUSE IS BACK!!!
LOOK! IT'S EXACTLY LIKE IT USED TO BE! THE KITCHEN WINDOW IS THE SAME! WOW!
AHHH, SQUIDWARD, ISN'T THIS GREAT? I'M BACK FOREVER!
FOREVER.
THE END

SpongeBob SquarePants™

F.U.N.

by Sherm Cohen, Aaron Springer and Peter Burns

THE KRUSTY KRAB
AHHH, LUNCHTIME AT THE KRUSTY KRAB.
EVERYONE'S ENJOYING THEIR KRABBY PATTIES.
HUH? WHAT'S THIS?
WOOP!
WOOP!
CAN YOU SPOT HIM, MR. SQUIDWARD?!
WOOP!
DOWN THERE, SIR!
WOOP!
CRASH!
KA-ZAP!

HAH!

THERE APPEARS TO BE A KRABBY PATTY-NAPPING IN PROGRESS.

THERE CAN BE ONLY ONE CULPRIT...

THE KRUSTY KRAB

PLANKTON.

FINALLY! VICTORY IS MINE!! I WIN! I WIN! I WIN!!!

PERHAPS NOT, MONSIEUR KRABS, FOR IT'S...

WOOSH!

KLANK!
HMMM
HUH?
AHA!
ZOOM!
HOLD IT RIGHT THERE!!!
KZZZOOP!
TARTAR SAUCE!!!
ZOOM!

WHIR!
WHIRRR
THUNK!
BLOOP!
HA!
BOING!

MAGIC SHOP

UH...HAVE YOU SEEN A KRABBY PATTY? IT'S ABOUT THIS TALL AND...

WOW! A MAGIC SHOP!

ARE YOU A MAGICIAN?!

ONE TIME I SAW THIS MAGICIAN AND HE TOOK THIS THING, AND HE... UH...ANYWAY! THEN HE TOLD US IF YOU BELIEVE IN YOURSELF...
...AND WITH A TINY PINCH OF MAGIC ALL YOUR DREAMS CAN COME TRUE!!

UGH!! I CAN'T TAKE IT!

PLANKTON! IT'S YOU!
YES, AND AFTER ALL THESE YEARS, I THOUGHT I WAS THE MASTER OF TORTURE!! BUT THAT...THAT JUST WASN'T FAIR!!
HERE! TAKE THE STUPID PATTY! I DON'T WANT THE SECRET RECIPE ANYWAY! I GUESS MY RESTAURANT WILL NEVER BE AS GOOD AS THE KRUSTY KRAB!
YOU DON'T KNOW WHAT IT'S LIKE TO BE A LOSER!
SOB!
AW— CHEER UP, PLANKTON. I THINK YOU'RE A WINNER!
SOB!
W-WHAT DID YOU JUST SAY?
I SAID YOU'RE A...

LOSER!

HOW DOES IT FEEL TO BE THE MOST HATED THING IN BIKINI BOTTOM, PLANKTON?! IT HURTS, DOESN'T IT?! I KNOW.
SOB!

YEAH! AND FOR RUNNING HIM OUT, WE'RE GONNA MAKE THIS KID HONORARY TOWN ROOKIE OF THE DAY!!

FOR HE'S A JOLLY GOOD ROOO-KIE, FOR HE'S A JOLLY GOOD ROOO-KIE!

FOR HE'S A JOLLY GOOD ROOKIE...
WOOSH!

WOOSH!

I BET IF HE HAD JUST ONE FRIEND, HE WOULDN'T BE SUCH A MEANIE!

DING-DONG
A CUSTOMER!
Hi, MR. PLANKTON!
HAVEN'T YOU DEGRADED ME ENOUGH FOR ONE DAY?
NO. i MEAN, i WANT YOU TO COME OUT AND PLAY WiTH ME.
YOU KNOW HOW TO iNDUCE THERMONUCLEAR FUSiON?
NO, BUT i LiKE TO GO JELLYF—
SLAM!
THAT NAiVE CUBE!
HOW LONG MUST i SUFFER THiS...

YOU'RE NOT LETTING HIM LEAVE, ARE YOU? CAN'T YOU SEE THIS IS THE PERFECT OPPORTUNITY FOR REVENGE?!
BEFRIEND THE SPONGEBOB, THEN, WHEN THE TIMING IS JUST RIGHT...
TAKE THE KRABBY PATTY!
GET MOVING, GENIUS! DON'T LET HIM GET AWAY!
—ISHING WITH MY FRIENDS IN JELLYFISH FIELDS!
ALL RIGHT, SPONGEBOB, I'LL PLAY YOUR LITTLE GAME!
GREAT! LAST ONE TO THE FIELDS IS A ROTTEN CLAM!

SO I GET THE BIG NET, AND YOU GET THE LITTLE NET.

WHAT HAPPENS AFTER WE EAT 'EM?

KOOOOSH!

YOU DON'T EAT 'EM! YOU CATCH 'EM, LIKE THIS!

...AND?!

...THEN YOU THROW 'EM BACK!

BLUB!

BUT WATCH OUT FOR THE STINGERS!

STINGERS?

ALL WILL BOW TO PLANKTON! HAIL PLANKTON! I WIN! I WIN!

KZZ-ZAP!

WHAT'S THAT?
FUN IS WHEN... FUN IS... IT'S LIKE... IT'S KINDA, SORTA LIKE... WHAT IS FUN LIKE? LET ME SPELL IT FOR YOU.
"F" IS FOR FRIENDS WHO DO STUFF TOGETHER...
"U" IS FOR YOU AND MEEEEEE...
"N" IS FOR ANYWHERE AND ANYTIME AT ALL! DOWN HERE IN THE DEEP BLUE SEEEEEEEEEA!
"F" IS FOR FIRE! THAT BURNS DOWN THE WHOLE TOWN!
"U" IS FOR URANIUM... BOMBS!
"N" IS FOR...NO SURVIVORS! WHEN YOU...
PLANKTON! THOSE THINGS AREN'T WHAT FUN IS ALL ABOUT. NOW DO IT LIKE THIS!

"F" IS FOR FRIENDS WHO DO STUFF...
NEVER! THAT'S COMPLETELY IDIOTIC!
HERE, LET ME HELP YOU. "F" IS FOR FRIENDS WHO DO STUFF TOGETHER...
"U" IS FOR YOU AND ME... TRY IT!
"N" IS FOR ANYWHERE AND ANYTIME AT ALL.
DOWN HERE IN THE DEEP BLUE SEA!
WAIT! I DON'T UNDERSTAND THIS! I FEEL ALL TINGLY INSIDE. SHOULD WE STOP?

NO, THAT'S HOW YOU'RE SUPPOSED TO FEEL!

WELL, I LIKE IT! LET'S DO IT AGAIN!
"F" IS FOR FRO-LIC THROUGH ALL THE FLOWERS... "U" IS FOR UKULELE...
FUN
HA! HA!
HA! HA!
FUN
HA! HA!
N
"N" IS FOR NOSE-PICKING, SHARING GUM AND SAND LICKING... HERE WITH MY BEST BUD-DY.
FUN
ARRRRR! MUTINY!

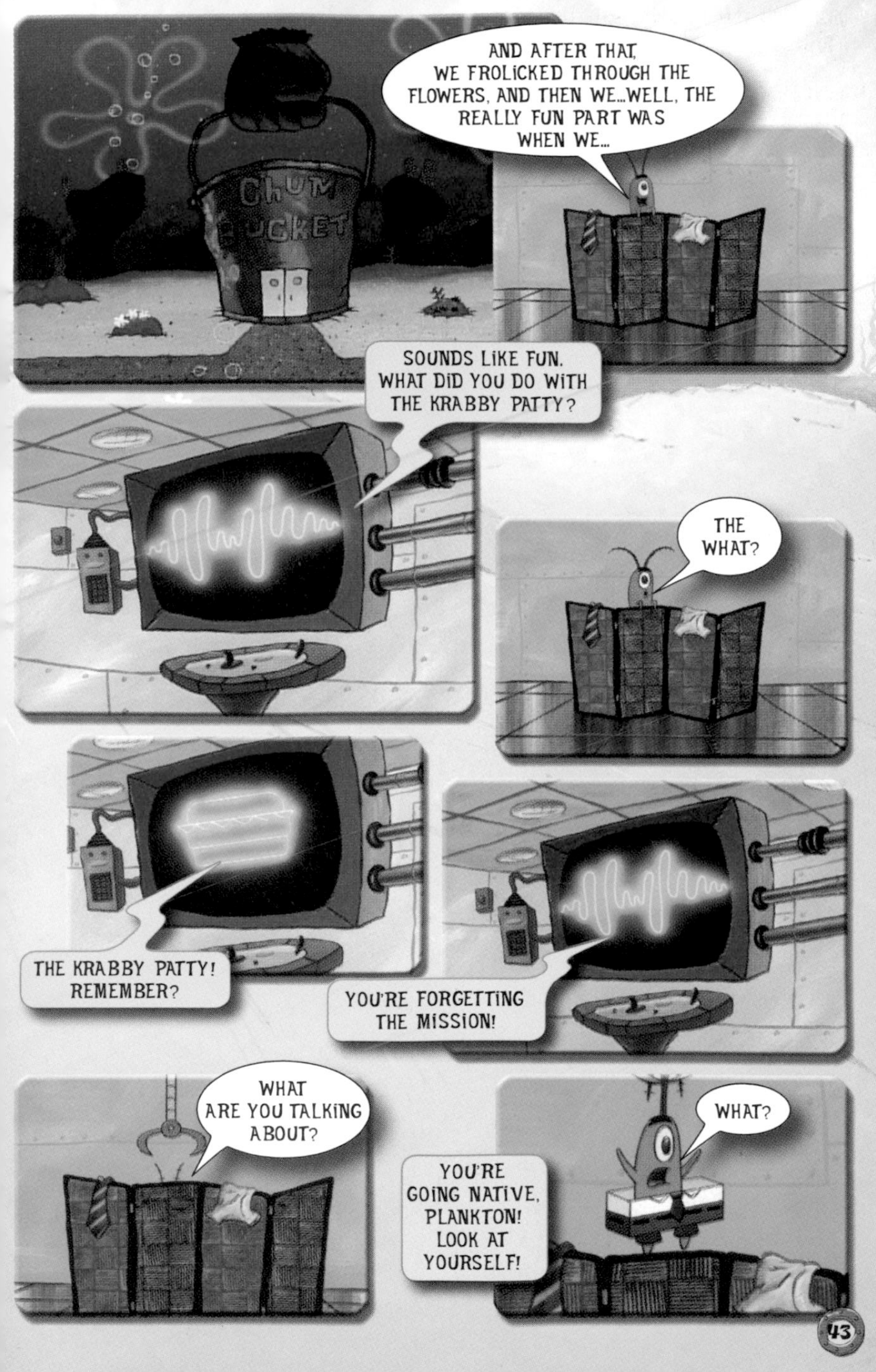
CHUM BUCKET
AND AFTER THAT, WE FROLICKED THROUGH THE FLOWERS, AND THEN WE...WELL, THE REALLY FUN PART WAS WHEN WE...
SOUNDS LIKE FUN. WHAT DID YOU DO WITH THE KRABBY PATTY?
THE WHAT?
THE KRABBY PATTY! REMEMBER?
YOU'RE FORGETTING THE MISSION!
WHAT ARE YOU TALKING ABOUT?
WHAT?
YOU'RE GOING NATIVE, PLANKTON! LOOK AT YOURSELF!

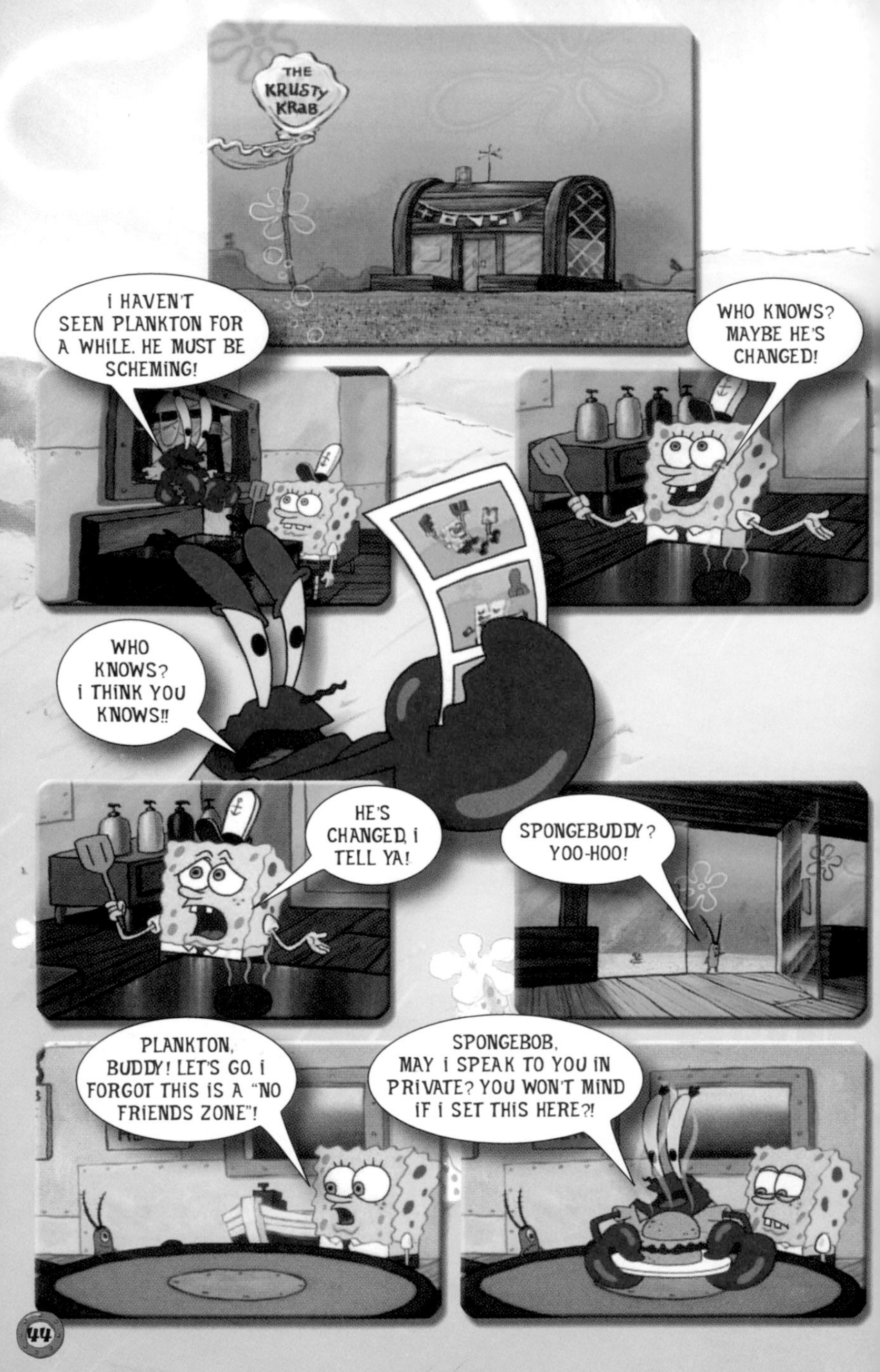
THE KRUSTY KRAB
i HAVEN'T SEEN PLANKTON FOR A WHiLE. HE MUST BE SCHEMiNG!
WHO KNOWS? MAYBE HE'S CHANGED!
WHO KNOWS? i THiNK YOU KNOWS!!
HE'S CHANGED, i TELL YA!
SPONGEBUDDY? YOO-HOO!
PLANKTON, BUDDY! LET'S GO. i FORGOT THiS iS A "NO FRiENDS ZONE"!
SPONGEBOB, MAY i SPEAK TO YOU iN PRiVATE? YOU WON'T MiND iF i SET THiS HERE?!

ORDER HERE
WHAT'S THIS ALL ABOUT, MR. KRABS?
HE'S A THIEF! LOOK AT THE LUST IN HIS EYE! HE'S...
WHY CAN'T YOU JUST ACCEPT OUR FRIENDSHIP?
ORDER HERE
HE'S JUST AFTER MY RECIPE. I'LL PROVE IT TO YA!
ARR! YOU MUST BE HUNGRY AFTER THAT LONG WALK OVER HERE.
OH, YES, BUT I'M SAVING MY APPETITE FOR SOME POPCORN AT THE MOVIES!
WE'VE HAD ENOUGH OF YOUR LITTLE TESTS, MR. KRABS! C'MON, PLANKTON, LET'S GET OUT OF HERE.
ORDER HERE
MAYBE THE LAD WAS RIGHT. MAYBE PLANKTON'S GONE STRAIGHT...
THUNK!
MAYBE SCALLOPS WILL FLY OUT OF MY PANTS! HANG ON THERE, LADDY! I'M A-COMIN'!

I SURE LIKE SEQUELS, PLANKTON!

LISTEN UP!!

WHAT IS IT THEN? TELL ME WHAT YOU SEE HERE?!
I-I DON'T SEE ANYTHING!
SOB!
HOW CAN YOU NOT SEE IT?
OKAY, OKAY! I SEE IT!! IT'S A KRABBY PATTY, OKAY?!!! I COULDN'T HELP IT!!!
SOB!
BUT WE SANG THE FUN SONG. I THINK I'M GOING TO BE SICK.
ALL RIGHT! IT'S TRUE! I TRICKED YOU TO GET TO THE KRABBY PATTY!! BUT THEN YOU SHOWED ME FRIENDSHIP...
...AND NOW I REALIZE... THAT'S ALL I EVER REALLY WANTED.
SOB!
REALLY?!
NO— NOT REALLY! BEING EVIL IS TOO MUCH FUN!
RIP!
MR. KRABS, HE'S GONE. HE GOT THE PATTY. HE WON.

NO, HE DIDN'T, BOY! DON'T YOU KNOW WHAT'S BEHIND THESE SCREENS? SOLID CONCRETE! AH HA HA HA!
UGH!
I'M SORRY, MR. KRABS. I THOUGHT PLANKTON HAD CHANGED.
DON'T BLAME HIM, LAD. NO FRIENDSHIP CAN WITHSTAND THE ALLURE OF A KRABBY PATTY. NOW, LET'S GO BACK TO THE KRUSTY KRAB AND HAVE A FRESH ONE ON ME!
AYE-AYE, MR. KRABS!
WELL, MAYBE AT A DISCOUNT.
FLICK
WOOSH!
YEAAAAAAAAAHH!
THE END

PreHiberNation WEEK

by Aaron Springer, C.H. Greenblatt and Merriwether Williams

THERE WE GO! HEY, SPONGEBOB! I GOT ALL THE LEAVES RAKED.
TEXAS
SPONGEBOB! WHAT ARE ALL THESE LEAVES DOING HERE?! YOU SAID YOU WERE GONNA RAKE 'EM!
I AM RAKING THE LEAVES.
BUT THEY'RE STILL ALL OVER THE GROUND!
SANDY, I CAN'T RAKE ANY FASTER! THESE ARE BIG LEAVES! AND THEY KEEP BREAKING INTO MORE LEAVES!
SCRITCH
SCRITCH
THEN GO SCRAPE THE SALT LICK OR SOMETHIN'! WE GOTTA GET THIS STUFF DONE BEFORE IT'S TOO LATE.
WHAT'S THE BIG RUSH ANYWAY, SANDY?

I TOLD YA, SPONGEBOB... I'M HIBERNATING NEXT WEEK!
HIBERNATING? WHAT'S THAT?
IT'S WHEN I GO TO SLEEP FOR THE WHOLE WINTER!
WASHA WASHA!
CAN I DO THAT?
NO, SILLY! IT'S A MAMMALIAN THING!
SANDY, YOU MAY NOT HAVE NOTICED... BUT I IS 100% MA-MALE!
ENOUGH CHITTER-CHATTER, SPONGEBOB, WE DON'T HAVE MUCH TIME LEFT!
WHY, SANDY?
MONDAY
TUESDAY
WHEN DOES YOUR CARBURATION BEGIN?
IN ONE WEEK!

BUT SANDY, THAT ONLY GIVES US 168 MORE HOURS OF PLAYTIME!
YOU'RE TELLIN' ME! AND THERE'S STILL SO MUCH TO DO! WE GOTTA CLIMB SOME THINGS.
CLIMB!
WE GOTTA JUMP OFFA STUFF
JUMP!
WE GOTTA RIDE!
RIDE.
I DON'T WANNA GO TO SLEEP YET!
WAIT, SANDY!
I CAN'T BURN CARBS IN MY SLEEP!
SANDY, I'M WILLING TO SACRIFICE ANY OF MY TIME THAT I HAVEN'T ALREADY SOLD TO MR. KRABS TO YOU.
WELL, I'M GLAD, SPONGEBOB, CAUSE FOR THE NEXT SEVEN DAYS, IT'S GONNA BE YOU, ME AND THESE SWEATBANDS!

SAND
MOUNTAiN
YEE-HAW!!
SWOOSH
GLINT?
ZLAAASH!
i AM HOTTER THAN A HiCKORY-SMOKED SAUSAGE!
BLAAASH!
BLAAASH!
MAYBE iF WE SiNG THAT SONG, HE'LL COME TO LiFE!

YAAAAAAHH!

THWACK!

YEAH! WHEW! WHAT A WORKOUT!

I'M GONNA BE FEELING THIS TOMORROW. OW.

I GOTTA SAY, I'M IMPRESSED WITH YOU, SPONGEBOB!

YER MAKIN' THIS THE BEST PRE-HIBERNATION WEEK EVER!

WELL, I'D BETTER GET HOME BEFORE GARY CHEWS UP THE SOFA AGAIN.

UGH!
OW!

GOODNIGHT, GARY!
SPROING!
EEEYYAAAAAH!
SPLASH
WOO-HOO! NOTHIN' LIKE A REFRESHING MORNING DIP, EH, SPONGEBOB?!
W-W-WHAT H-H-HAPPENED TO SLEEPING?
I'LL BE ASLEEP ALL WINTER! WE ONLY GOT THREE DAYS FOR FUN!

OKAY, SPONGEBOB, THIS ONE'S GONNA BE FUN! WE JUST WHACK EACH OTHER WITH THESE GIANT EAR CLEANERS TILL ONE OF US FALLS OFF!

SANDY, ARE YOU SURE WE'RE SUPPOSED TO BE STANDING UP HERE?

ON YOUR MARK...GET SET...GO!

SEA NEEDLE

C'MON, SPONGEBOB! WE'RE GOIN' FOR A TANDEM RIDE THROUGH THE PARK.

GEE, THAT SOUNDS SAFE. I MEAN, FUN!

OKAY, I'M READY.

YEAH!

I THOUGHT YOU SAID WE WERE RIDING THROUGH THE PARK, SANDY!
I DID, SPONGEBOB. THE INDUSTRIAL PARK! THIS IS WHERE THE REAL ACTION IS!! C'MON, PEDAL!!
THIS PART GETS PRETTY TECHNICAL! YEE-HAW!
CLOMP!
CLOMP!
CLOMP!
NOW FOR THE SPEED COURSE! HANG ON!
ARRRRGGGGHHHH...
I HOPE WE MAKE IT.
CRASH!
CRASH!

UGH!
THIS SQUIRREL'S TRYING TO KILL ME!
GLUG!
GLUG!
WAKE UP, SLOWPOKE! WE'RE GOING FLY-FISHIN'.
ANY MORE OF THESE STUNTS AND I'LL BE REDUCED TO A PUDDLE!
WAIT A MINUTE—I GOTTA TALK MY WAY OUT OF THIS!
SANDY, I THINK I NEED TO TELL YOU SOMETHING.
WHAT IS IT?
WELL, IT'S JUST THAT I'M FEELING SORT OF DRAINED AND SO I DON'T THINK I CAN... BLUB, BLUB... I JUST FEEL LIKE MAYBE I NEED TO...
HOLD THAT THOUGHT, SPONGEBOB...
'CAUSE IT'S TIME FOR A DOWN-HOME FAVORITE! FIND THE HAY IN THE NEEDLE STACK!
FLINK!

OUCH.
DID YA FIND IT?!
NOT YET!
WELL, I'M GONNA LOOK OVER HERE!
YOU DO THAT.
PANT!
PANT!
FOUND IT, SPONGEBOB! COME ON! BEST TWO OUTTA THREE!
GOTTA HIDE! GOTTA HIDE!
HOME? NO! GARY CAN'T KEEP A SECRET!
UNDER A ROCK? IT'S SO ORIGINAL!

SPROING!

THUNK!

BOINK!

SHLLLP

BLINK!
SPONGEBOB? SPONGEBOOOOOB? WHERE ARE YOU, LITTLE SQUARE DUDE?
SPONGEBOB'S TIE! AND ALL HIS OTHER LITTLE DRESSIN'S!

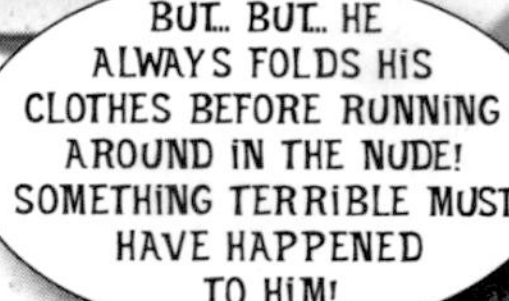
BUT... BUT... HE ALWAYS FOLDS HIS CLOTHES BEFORE RUNNING AROUND IN THE NUDE! SOMETHING TERRIBLE MUST HAVE HAPPENED TO HIM!

GASP!

ALL RIGHT! LISTEN UP, Y'ALL!
I'M ROUNDIN' UP A SEARCH PARTY! SPONGEBOB'S GONE MISSIN'!
MAN THE LIFEBOATS!
ALPHA TEAM, YOU SEARCH UPTOWN! GOLD TEAM SEARCHES DOWNTOWN.
NOW GET MOVIN'!
THE KRUSTY KRAB
LOST
PAT!
PAT!
SPONGEBOB!
SPONGEBOB!

C'MON! HE COULD BE ANYWHERE IN THESE SULFUR FIELDS!
HEY, SPONGEBOB?
WOOSH!
WELL, AT LEAST I STILL HAVE MY PERSONALITY.
CHECK IN THIS HERE MOIST CAVE!
SPONGEBOB? SPONGEBOB? YOU IN HERE?
GLUG!
GLUG!
AAAAAAAA!

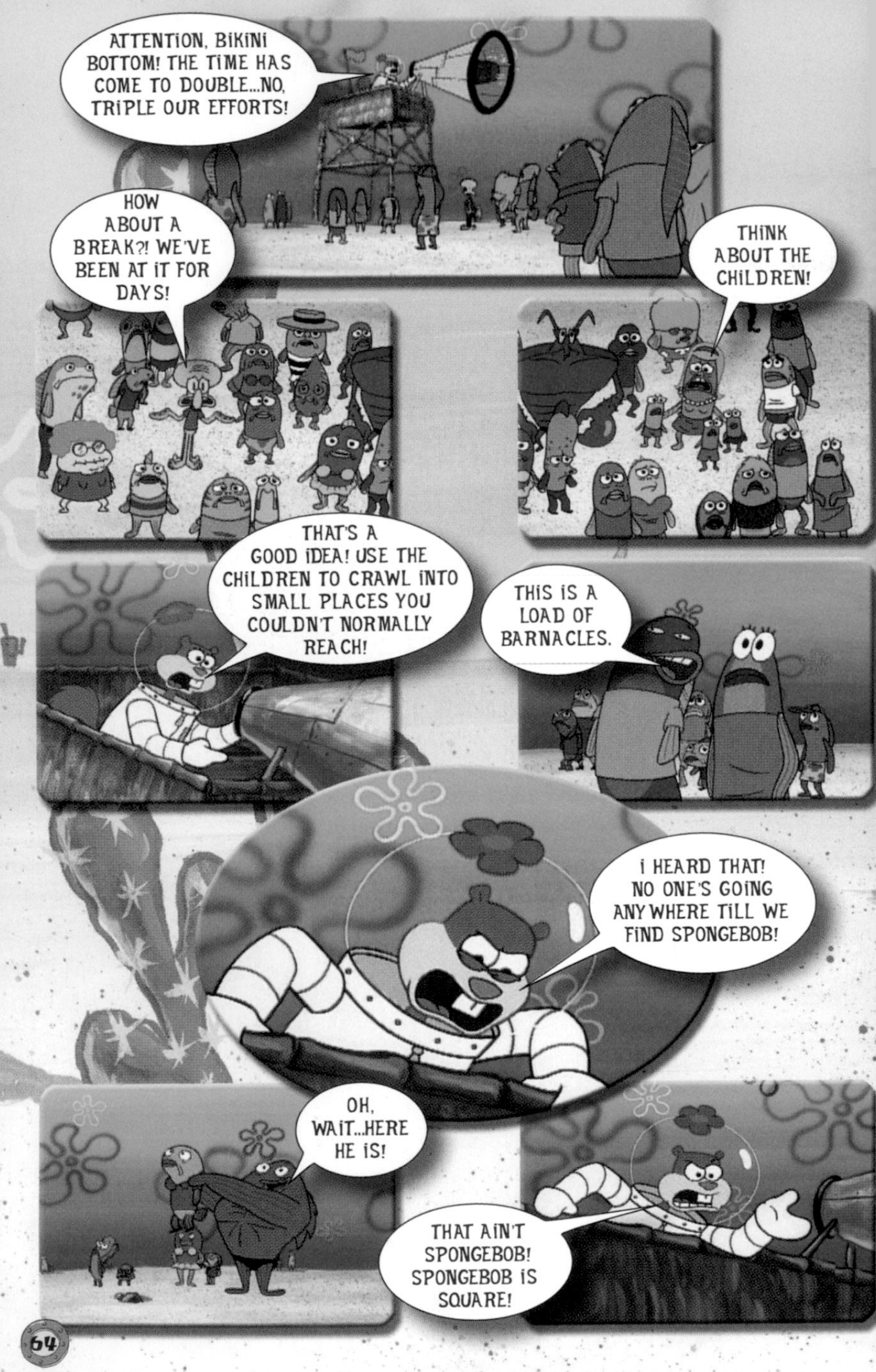
ATTENTION, BIKINI BOTTOM! THE TIME HAS COME TO DOUBLE...NO, TRIPLE OUR EFFORTS!
HOW ABOUT A BREAK?! WE'VE BEEN AT IT FOR DAYS!
THINK ABOUT THE CHILDREN!
THAT'S A GOOD IDEA! USE THE CHILDREN TO CRAWL INTO SMALL PLACES YOU COULDN'T NORMALLY REACH!
THIS IS A LOAD OF BARNACLES.
I HEARD THAT! NO ONE'S GOING ANYWHERE TILL WE FIND SPONGEBOB!
OH, WAIT...HERE HE IS!
THAT AIN'T SPONGEBOB! SPONGEBOB IS SQUARE!

I FOUND SQUAREBOB!
KELPO
THAT'S JUST A CEREAL BOX! 'SIDES, HE'S YELLOW!
HERE HE IS! CAN I GO HOME NOW?!
GRRRRR!!!
OH LOOK! HE'S UP IN THE SKY!
HE'S NOT...
HUH?
THEY MUST'VE GONE TO SEARCH SOME MORE!
BLINK!
BLINK!

SPONGEBOB?!
SPONGEBOB!! WHERE ARE YOU?!
YOU UNDER THERE?! NOPE!
THWANK!
NOPE!
THWANK!
SPONGEBOB!! WHERE ARE YOU?!
SPONGEBOB!!
THAT SQUIRREL'S GONE CRAZY!

BUT SHE'LL NEVER LOOK UNDER A ROCK!
HAAA! YOU SAID IT! SANDY'LL NEVER FIND US!
GASP!
HEY, WAIT! YOU DON'T UNDERSTAND!
HMPH!
OH LOOK, IT IS I, SPONGEBOB, OUT HERE IN THE OPEN.
COME ON, LET ME BACK IN!
SPONGEBOB?
YANK!
OH, SPONGEBOB! I WAS SOOO WORRIED! I THOUGHT SOMETHIN' TERRIBLE HAPPENED!
C'MON! THERE'S JUST ENOUGH TIME TO GO ATOM SMASHING!

SANDY, WAIT!
THERE'S NO TIME TO WAIT! HIBERNATION!
SANDY, YOU GOTTA MAKE TIME! THIS IS IMPORTANT!
OKAY, SANDY, I CAN'T PLAY WITH YOU ANY MORE! I JUST CAN'T TAKE THE GAMES! THEY'RE TEARING ME APART!!
THERE, I SAID IT. NOW JUST PROMISE WE CAN STILL BE FRIENDS. PLEASE, SANDY? THIS ISN'T EASY.
ZZZZZ!
SANDY? HA! I NEVER THOUGHT I'D SAY IT, BUT THANK NEPTUNE FOR HIBERNATION! AAAAAAAA!
HA! HA! HA!
ZZZZZ!
THE END

I'm Your Biggest Fanatic

by Jay Lender, William Reiss and Mr. Lawrence

WELCOME JELLYFISHERS

WOW! I CAN'T BELIEVE IT! WE'RE ACTUALLY HERE AT THE BIANNUAL JELLYFISH AND VINTAGE CAR CONVENTION!

JELLYFISH ARE AWESOME!

LOOK! DR. MANOWAR! THE GUY WHO GOT STUNG BY BIG LENNY AND LIVED.
AND NOW IT ONLY HURTS WHEN YOU TOUCH IT.
TOUCH.
AAAH!!
DO I HAVE TO FOLLOW YOU ALL DAY?
EEEEEEEEK!! LOOK! CAN IT BE?
ICE CREAM?
NO, IT'S THE JELLY SPOTTERS, BIKINI BOTTOM'S PREMIERE JELLYFISH ENTHUSIAST CLUB, AND THEIR LEADER, THE COOLEST JELLYFISH ENTHUSIAST EVER, KEVIN THE SEA CUCUMBER.
The JELLYSPOTTERS
Kevin's OINTMENT

WHAT'S SO GREAT ABOUT A NERDY PICKLE?

IF I COULD JUST TOUCH THE HEM OF HIS POCKET PROTECTOR, THEN MAYBE SOME OF HIS GREATNESS WOULD RUB OFF ON ME!

OH MY GOSH, JEFFREY JELLYFISH! WAIT, JEFFREY, I HAVE TO TOUCH YOU!

BAMBOO?
I ONLY USE COMPOSITE MATERIALS IN MY NET HANDLE.
COMPOSITE MATERIALS...
COMPOSITE MATERIALS...
SCRIBBLE!
NEXT QUESTION?
HI, WHAT IS YOUR QUESTION?
UHHH, HI, KEVIN.
HI, KEVIN.
WHATEVER. NEXT QUESTION, PLEASE.

HI, KEVIN.
HELLO, LOSER. ALL RIGHT, YOU, WAY IN THE BACK.
HI, KEVIN.
DOES ANYONE HERE HAVE AN ACTUAL...
HI, KEVIN. I'M YOUR BIGGEST FAN.
YOU'RE TOO KIND.
SECURITY!
NO, WAIT! I WOULD DO ANYTHING FOR YOU.

WHY DON'T YOU GO JUMP OFF A BUILDING?
The ELLYSPOTTERS
The ELLYSPOTTERS
ANYTHING...
PUNCH YOURSELF IN THE FACE.
WHAP!
DOESN'T THAT HURT YOU?
DO YOU WANT IT TO HURT ME, KEVIN?

HA! HA! HA!
THAT'S THE BEST! THIS GUY'S GREAT!
WE GOTTA BRING THIS GUY JELLYFISHING WITH US!

KEVIN, NO! HE'S A GEEK!
MEEP! MEEP!
LOOK, I WON'T LET THE GUY JOIN THE CLUB, I JUST WANNA SEE HOW MANY TIMES HE CAN GET STUNG BEFORE HE GOES RUNNING HOME LIKE A BABY.

KEVIN'S A GENIUS! WE LOVE KEVIN!
HEY KID, HOW'D YOU LIKE TO TRY OUT FOR THE JELLY SPOTTERS?

CLEAR.

I'D LOVE IT!
WHAAAZZZ!

NOTHING LIKE DRIVING THROUGH JELLYFISH FIELDS WITH THE TOP DOWN, EH, JELLY SPOTTERS?
TOP DOWN!
MEEP!
MEEP!
HERE WE ARE, JELLYFISH FIELDS.
JellyFish FIELDS
I HOPE YOU DIDN'T FORGET OUR NETS!
I DIDN'T FORGET THEM, KEVIN. THEY'RE IN THE TRUNK!
I CAN'T BELIEVE I'M OUT HERE WITH THE JELLY SPOTTERS! I MEAN, ALL MY LIFE I WANTED TO BE A JELLY SPOTTER AND NOW I'M OUT HERE WITH YOU GUYS...

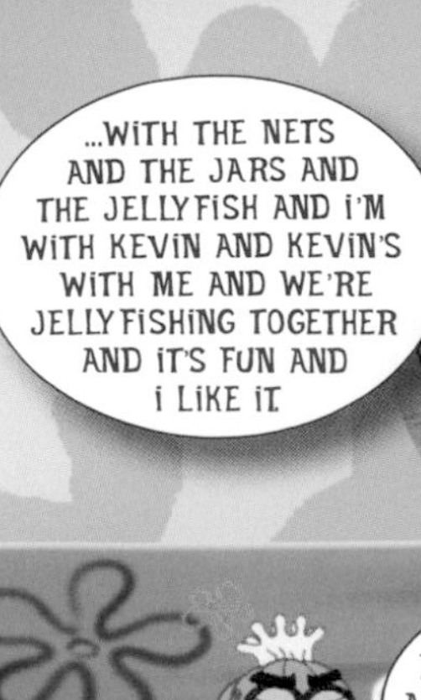

...WITH THE NETS AND THE JARS AND THE JELLYFISH AND I'M WITH KEVIN AND KEVIN'S WITH ME AND WE'RE JELLYFISHING TOGETHER AND IT'S FUN AND I LIKE IT.

HOLD IT! BEFORE YOU BECOME A JELLY SPOTTER, YOU HAVE TO PASS A RIGOROUS TEST.

TEE
HEE
HEE
MEEP!
MEEP!

QUIET! SHHHH!

YOUR FIRST TEST IS TO CATCH A JELLYFISH.

HEY, I CAUGHT ONE! AM I A JELLY SPOTTER NOW?
PLOP

HE CAUGHT ONE. IN THE CLUB?
THAT DOESN'T COUNT.
SMACK!

BZZZ-ZAP!

OUCH!

I MEANT TWO JELLYFISH.

PLOP

TWO JELLYFISH! IN THE NET.

FLOOSH!

OWWWW!!!
BZZZ-ZAP!

OW!

JELLY SPOTTERS ALLOW JELLYFISH TO EAT JELLY OFF THEIR FACE.

SMEAR!
SMOOSH!
SMAP!

WHO WANTS TO LICK MY CHEEKS? I SEE I HAVE SOME TAKERS.

HOW DOES IT FEEL?

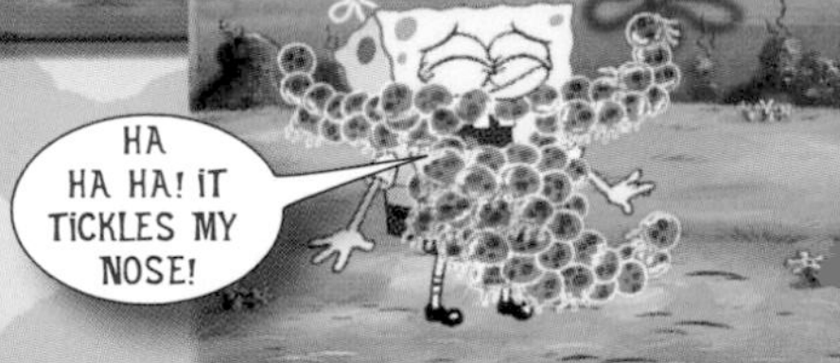
HA HA HA! IT TICKLES MY NOSE!

NOT FOR LONG! HA HA HA!
HA-CHOO!
BZZZ-ZAP!
AM I IN THE JELLY SPOTTERS NOW?
NO..
I HAVE ONE FINAL TEST FOR YOU TO TAKE!

THIS IS FANTASTIC! I'VE NEVER BEEN BAIT BEFORE! I DON'T THINK I'VE EVER SEEN A QUEEN JELLYFISH, EITHER.

WELL, THEN YOU'VE PROBABLY NEVER USED A QUEEN JELLYFISH CALL.

WHY DON'T YOU TRY IT OUT.

LOSER! LOSER!

HEY! ITH HEARD THITH CALL BETHAW!

I'LL BET YOU HAVE.

OUCH! WHO'S GOT MY STING OINTMENT?
THIS IS GREAT! WHEN I PASS THIS TEST, I'LL BE AN OFFICIAL JELLY SPOTTER!
LOSER! LOSER!
LOSER! LOSER!
HEY, KEVIN. I DON'T THINK IT'S WORKING. NOTHING'S...
HUH?

HEY! HEY, KEVIN! SHE'S HERE! LOOK! LOOK! SHE'S HERE! SHE'S HERE! SHE'S HERE, KEVIN. SHE'S...

WOOSH!

GASP!

AAAAAAAAA!

AAAH!
BZZZ-ZAP!

BZZZ ZAP!

BZZZ
PLEASE DON'T BE ANGRY, YOUR HIGHNESS! I WOULD HAVE LET YOU GO!
HA! HA! HA! HA! HA!
KEVIN!
THAT'S RIGHT! YOU SHOULD HAVE SEEN THE LOOK ON YOUR FACE WHEN WE ZAPPED YOU!
BUT WHAT ABOUT MY FINAL TEST?
DID YOU THINK WE'D ACTUALLY LET YOU JOIN THE JELLY SPOTTERS?
BUT, KEVIN! I WAS YOUR BIGGEST FAN!
SO WERE THEY!

HEY, LOOK, EVERYBODY! KEVIN'S BACK!
KEVIN! WE LOVE YOU, KEVIN!

YOU LOOKED SO DUMB WITH YOUR DORKY JELLYFISH CALL!

SNIFF

LOSER! LOSER! LOSER! LOSER!

I'M NOT A LOSER.
LOOOOOOOOOOOOOOOSER!

LOSER!
LOSER!
LOSER!
HA!
HA!
HA!

CNYDARIA REX!
GASP!

KING JELLYFISH!

KISSY
KISSY
KISSY

KISSY
YAH!

GOT STUNG? USE KEVIN'S OINTMENT KEVIN'S Favorite!
AAAH!

CRASH!

HUH?

HMMM

OOHHH OOHH..

BZZZ-ZAP!

AAAH!

DON'T LOOK AT ME! I WAS JUST IN THIS FOR THE FASHION!
IT'S HOPELESS. WE'RE TRAPPED. WE'RE TRAPPED. HELP ME, MOMMY. HELP ME.
HMMM
WHAT THE...?
BZZZ
WOOSH!
PLIP!

HUH?
MMMMMMMMMM!!
YUMMY!

I CAN'T
BELIEVE IT! HOW
DID YOU KNOW?
HA HA!
EVERY BODY
LOVES PIE!
WELL, SQUAREPANTS,
THAT WAS IMPRESSIVE, BUT
YOU'RE STILL NOT IN THE CLUB
BECAUSE YOU DIDN'T CATCH
A QUEEN JELLYFISH.

WAIT, WHAT
ARE YOU
DOING?
RIP!
AAAH!

WOW! I
DIDN'T KNOW
THIS WAS A
HAT!
IT
WASN'T.

WELCOME JELLYFISHERS
HI PATRICK!
HI SPONGEBOB! DID YOU GET INTO THAT CLUB?
YEAH, BUT I TURNED THEM DOWN. IT'S NOT ABOUT KEVIN, IT'S ABOUT JELLYFISH.
SPONGEBOB, I'M GLAD YOU LEARNED YOUR LESSON. HERO WORSHIP IS UNHEALTHY.
C'MON, JEFFREY.
SQUISH!
SQUISH!
THE END

ALSO AVAILABLE FROM TOKYOPOP®

MANGA

.HACK//LEGEND OF THE TWILIGHT
ANGELIC LAYER
BABY BIRTH
BRAIN POWERED
BRIGADOON
B'TX
CANDIDATE FOR GODDESS, THE
CARDCAPTOR SAKURA
CARDCAPTOR SAKURA - MASTER OF THE CLOW
CHRONICLES OF THE CURSED SWORD
CLAMP SCHOOL DETECTIVES
CLOVER
COMIC PARTY
CORRECTOR YUI
COWBOY BEBOP
COWBOY BEBOP: SHOOTING STAR
CRESCENT MOON
CULDCEPT
CYBORG 009
D.N.ANGEL
DEMON DIARY
DEMON ORORON, THE
DIGIMON
DIGIMON ZERO TWO
DIGIMON TAMERS
DRAGON HUNTER
DRAGON KNIGHTS
DREAM SAGA
DUKLYON: CLAMP SCHOOL DEFENDERS
ET CETERA
ETERNITY
FAERIES' LANDING
FLCL
FORBIDDEN DANCE
FRUITS BASKET
G GUNDAM
GATE KEEPERS
GIRL GOT GAME
GUNDAM SEED ASTRAY
GUNDAM WING
GUNDAM WING: BATTLEFIELD OF PACIFISTS
GUNDAM WING: ENDLESS WALTZ
GUNDAM WING: THE LAST OUTPOST (G-UNIT)
HARLEM BEAT
I.N.V.U.
INITIAL D
JING: KING OF BANDITS
JULINE
KARE KANO
KILL ME, KISS ME
KINDAICHI CASE FILES, THE
KING OF HELL
KODOCHA: SANA'S STAGE
LEGEND OF CHUN HYANG, THE
MAGIC KNIGHT RAYEARTH I
MAGIC KNIGHT RAYEARTH II
MAN OF MANY FACES
MARMALADE BOY
MARS
MINK
MIRACLE GIRLS
MODEL
ONE
PEACH GIRL
PEACH GIRL: CHANGE OF HEART
PITA-TEN
PLANET LADDER
PLANETES
PRINCESS AI
PSYCHIC ACADEMY
RAGNAROK
RAVE MASTER
REALITY CHECK
REBIRTH
REBOUND
RISING STARS OF MANGA
SAILOR MOON
SAINT TAIL
SAMURAI GIRL REAL BOUT HIGH SCHOOL
SEIKAI TRILOGY, THE CREST OF THE STARS
SGT. FROG
SHAOLIN SISTERS
SHIRAHIME-SYO: SNOW GODDESS TALES
SKULL MAN, THE
SUIKODEN III
SUKI
THREADS OF TIME
TOKYO MEW MEW
VAMPIRE GAME
WISH
WORLD OF HARTZ
ZODIAC P.I.

01.09.04Y

FIND OUT IN THE NEW
the fairly OddParents!
NICKELODEON
CINE-MANGA